THIS BOOK BELONGS TO

....

....

FOR THE LITTLE TANGERINES, WHO INSPIRE ME EVERYDAY.

-B.W.

Hello, Friends! by Bola Williams

Illustration: Daniel A. Stevens Font: Cardenio Modern Bold.

Text & Illustration copyright © 2020 by Bola Williams

Pears lane Publishing is an imprint of Blue Thread, LLC

Visit www.pearslanepublishing.com

Printed in U.S.A

ISBN 978-1-7344484-1-2 (print)
ISBN 978-1-73444484-2-9 (ebook)

HELLO, FRIENDS!

WRITTEN BY
BOLA O. WILLIAMS

ILLUSTRATION BY
DANIEL A. STEVENS

Pears Lane Publishing
New York

GOING FOR A WALK IN MY NEIGHBORHOOD ALWAYS PUTS ME IN A GREAT MOOD.
I ESPECIALLY LOVE TO SEE MY FRIENDS AND SAY HELLO.

TODAY, I'M WALKING TO THE PARK WITH MY DAD. THERE'S A SUMMER PICNIC AND EVERYONE WILL BRING FOOD TO SHARE.

DAD SAID, "MAYBE WE'LL SEE SOME OF YOUR FRIENDS ALONG THE WAY, DANIEL. DON'T FORGET TO BRING YOUR APPLE PIE AND REMEMBER TO SAY HELLO!"

FIRST, I SEE MY FRIEND ZOLA. SHE SPEAKS FRENCH.
HELLO, ZOLA! I HAVE APPLE PIE.

BONJOUR, DANIEL! I HAVE A GÂTEAU.

NEXT, I SEE MY FRIEND MAI. SHE SPEAKS CHINESE.
HELLO, MAI! I HAVE APPLE PIE.

"Look up there, Daniel. Someone's waving at you." Pointed Dad. It's my friend Nia. She speaks Swahili. Hello, Nia! I have apple pie.

JAMBO, Daniel! I HAVE Kuku Choma

At the corner store, I see my friend Finn.
He's German. Hi, Finn! I have apple pie.

GUTEN TAG, Daniel! I HAVE DAS BROT.

"Hold my hand Daniel, we're going to cross the street now." Dad said. That's when I see my friend Hugo. He speaks Spanish. Hey, Hugo! I have apple pie.

HOLA, DANIEL! I HAVE FRIJOLES.

THIS IS MY FRIEND YUKI. HE SPEAKS JAPANESE.
HELLO, YUKI! I HAVE APPLE PIE.

DOWN THE STREET, I SEE MY FRIEND LISA. SHE SPEAKS ITALIAN. HI, LISA! I HAVE APPLE PIE.

CIAO, DANIEL! I HAVE GELATO.

Dad said, "We're almost there. Just a few more steps to go."
There's my friend Turner helping with the barbecue grill.
Hey, Turner! I have apple pie.

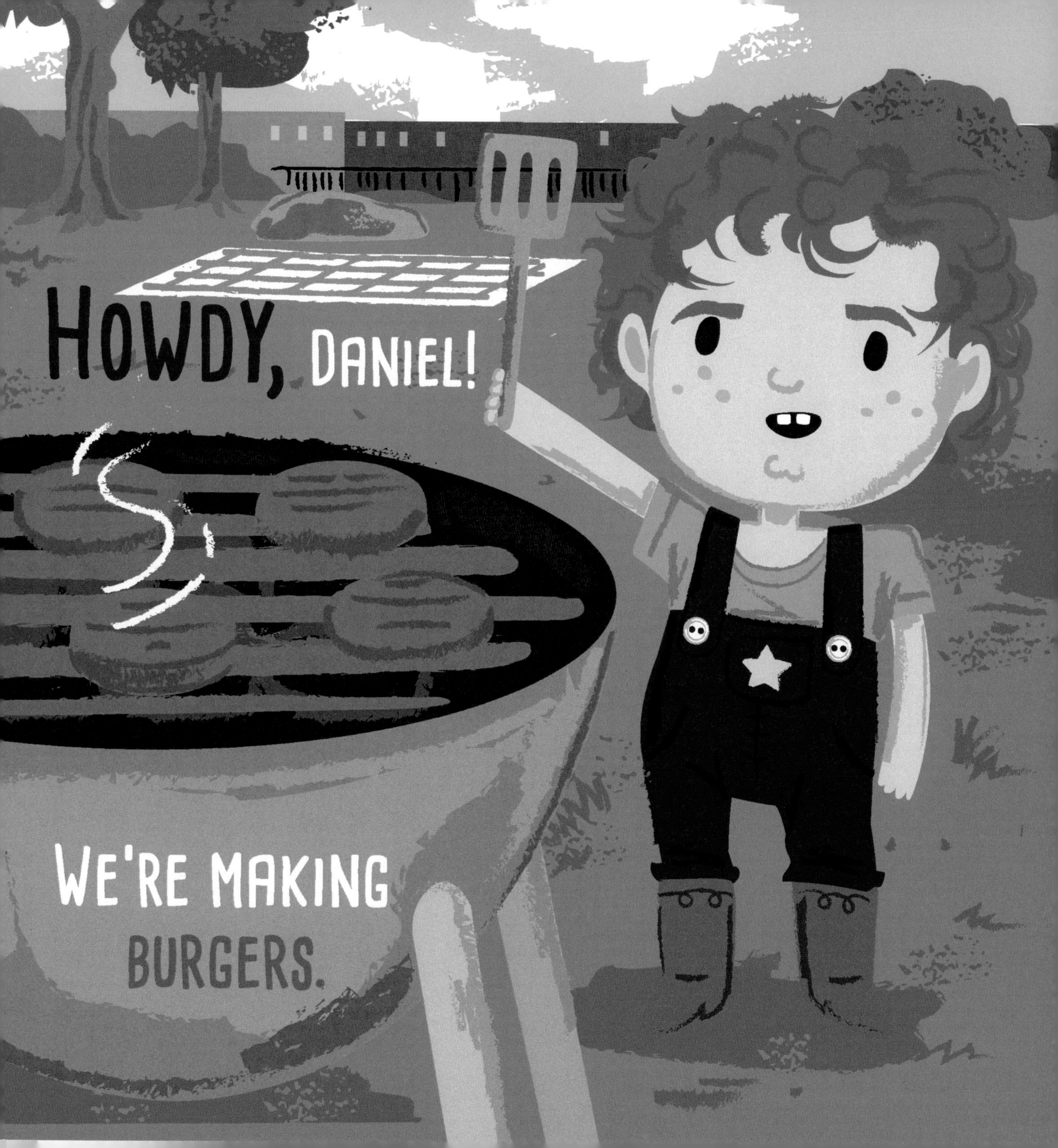

HOWDY, DANIEL!

WE'RE MAKING BURGERS.

WE'RE FINALLY AT THE PARK AND LOOK WHAT I SEE.

EVERYONE'S HERE AT THE SUMMER PICNIC PARTY.

PIE

MĬ FĂN

SELU

GÂTEAU

DAS BROT

Frijoles

Gelato

Burgers

Mikan

Kuku Choma

Our foods have different names but my friends and I are all the same.

HOWDY

CIAO

HI

IN MY NEIGHBORHOOD,
EACH AND EVERYDAY,

BONJOUR

NI-HAO

KON'NICHIWA

HOLA

WE ALL SAY HELLO IN
A DIFFERENT WAY.

GUTEN TAG

SIYO

JAMBO

THIS IS HOW TO SAY IT:

French
BONJOUR *bohn-zhoor*
GÂTEAU *ga-tow*

Mandarin (Chinese)
NI HAO *nee haow*
MǏ FǍN *mee fen*

Cherokee (Native American)
SIYO *see-yoh*
SELU *say-lu*

Swahili
JAMBO *jahm-boh*
KUKU CHOMA *kuku-cho-mah*

German
GUTEN TAG *goot-n-tahk*
DAS BROT *das-broat*

Spanish
HOLA *oh-la*
FRIJOLES *free-hoh-luhz*

Japanese
KON'NICHIWA *kohn-nee-che-wah*
MIKAN *me-kan*

Italian
CIAO *chow*
GELATO *gee-la-tow*

Western America
HOWDY
BURGER